# OFF
# THE MAP

Based on the series created by Dan Povenmire & Jeff "Swampy" Marsh

Adapted by

DISNEP PRESS
New York

Printed in the United States of America
First Edition
10 9 8 7 6 5 4 3 2 1
J689-1817-1-12228

Library of Congress Control Number: 2012941072
ISBN 978-1-4231-3733-7

For more Disney Press fun, visit www.disneybooks.com
Visit DisneyChannel.com

# Part ONE

The Flynn-Fletcher family van rumbled up the twisty mountain road, past pine trees and steep cliffs. Phineas and Ferb weren't worried, though. With their dad at the wheel, they were certain to stay five miles under the speed limit and follow proper driving procedures at all times.

"Hey, we're almost there!" Phineas said excitedly from the middle row of the van. He'd

3

been looking forward to this trip since the very first day of summer vacation. It was a yearly tradition for Phineas's grandparents to invite everyone to their mountain cabin for a weekend campout! From hiking through the woods to swimming in the lake, there was never a dull moment in the great outdoors. And since Phineas and Ferb wanted to make every minute of summer count, the campout fit in perfectly with their plans. So far, they had been on one awesome adventure after another. And Phineas had a feeling that this camping trip was going to be legendary.

"What's the first thing you're going to do at camp, Buford?" Phineas asked his friend.

Buford didn't even have to think about it. "Find a nerd, take his underpants, and run 'em up the flagpole," he replied with a devious grin. As the resident bully of Danville, Buford had a knack for causing mischief in any situation.

Phineas winced. "How about you, Isabella?" he called over his shoulder to the girl sitting behind him.

Isabella smiled from her seat. "The Fireside Girls and I are going to work on our Accomplishment Patches," she said.

"Accomplishment Patches! Yay!" cheered a bunch of Fireside Girls, who popped up from the back of the van. Ferb jumped, too. He blew on a squeaky whistle to add to the celebration. Everyone was superexcited about summer camp!

Everyone except for one person.

"How about you, sis?" Phineas asked his older sister, Candace. "What's the first thing you're going to do at camp?"

"First of all, it's not 'camp,'" Candace corrected him. "It's just Grandma and Grandpa's cabin, and it's boring."

"But we made T-shirts!" Phineas exclaimed, holding up his custom blue *Camp Phineas and Ferb* shirt.

Candace continued as if her younger brother hadn't even spoken. "Secondly, I don't like the outdoors, okay? I don't like bugs!"

Phineas suddenly looked down at the floor. "Are you even listening to me?" Candace snapped.

"I seem to have misplaced my ant farm," Phineas replied thoughtfully.

"Mom!" Candace whined.

"Yes, Candace?" their mother answered from the front seat of the van.

"Do I *have* to go to Grandma and Grandpa's?" Candace sighed.

Candace's father looked back at her in the rearview mirror. "Oh, I think it's rather sweet that Betty Joe and Grandpa Clyde invite you kids and all your friends every year," he said.

"But I'm not a kid!" Candace complained. "I'm a young adult. Can't I do something with you guys?"

"Of course you can, dear," her mom said

excitedly. "You can join us at the antiques symposium. This year's keynote address will debate shellac versus lacquer."

"Woo-hoo!" cried their father.

Candace sank back into her seat in defeat. "I'll take one of those shirts," she said to Phineas with a sigh. After her brother handed her a T-shirt, Candace cried into it. There was nothing else she could do, really. Between *Camp Phineas and Ferb* and the antiques symposium, she was literally bored to tears!

Just a few miles away, Grandpa Clyde and Grandma Betty Joe waited in front of their cabin. "Look! Oh, here they come now!" Grandma Betty Joe pointed to the Flynn-Fletcher van.

"Hey!" Grandpa Clyde greeted Phineas and his pet platypus, Perry, as they stepped out.

"Hiya, Grandpa!" Phineas grinned.

"And Turbo Ferbo!" Grandpa Clyde

exclaimed as Ferb climbed down from the van. "So, where's your sister?"

The boys looked around, but they didn't see Candace anywhere. Little did they know that the moment Candace had gotten out of the van, she had raced off to make a call on her cell phone.

But because they were so deep in the woods, she couldn't get any reception. She had climbed a ladder to the roof of her grandparents' cabin hoping she could get a signal from there.

"Hello? Hello?!" Candace shouted over and over into her phone.

"Candace?" Grandma Betty Joe called.

"Oh, hi, Grandma," Candace replied. "How can you stand living out here in the middle of nowhere?"

"Oh, come on, honey. It's not so bad. You'll see," Grandma Betty Joe said.

Over on the other side of the clearing, Grandpa Clyde was gathering the campers. "All right, nature lovers!" Grandpa Clyde's voice boomed as he rang a chime. "Time for vittles!"

"'Vittles' is 'Grandpa-ese' for food," Phineas explained to Isabella. Then, he looked around. "Hey, where's Perry?"

The platypus seemed to have disappeared. That wasn't unusual, though. Perry often vanished—only to turn up again hours later.

But if Phineas and Ferb had known what

Perry was *really* up to, they would have skipped Grandpa Clyde's vittles in a heartbeat. After all, Perry was off on an adventure of his own!

**Chapter TWO**

Perry the Platypus hid behind the thick trunk of an oak tree and watched as the campers headed toward the cabin. He had to be careful. He couldn't risk anyone discovering that behind his guise as an ordinary pet platypus, he was actually a top secret agent! Known as Agent P to his fellow operatives, Perry had dedicated his life to fighting crime. His most dangerous nemesis was an evil scientist named Dr. Heinz Doofenshmirtz.

The moment the last camper disappeared from sight, Agent P slipped on his sleek fedora and knocked softly on an oak tree. A secret panel in the trunk creaked open.

Agent P wasted no time. He leaped into the hollow tree, crossed his arms tightly over his chest, and zoomed down a steep slide. It led straight to an underground briefing room. But as he slid, Agent P plunged through a mess of dusty old cobwebs! At the bottom of the slide,

a door opened—and the platypus crashed right into a decorative table with a vase on top!

"Sorry about that, Agent P," his boss, Major Monogram, said.

Agent P ran across the room and jumped into a captain's chair that faced a large flat-screen monitor on which Major Monogram was speaking.

"We haven't used that tree slide in years," the commander continued. "Not since I was at . . . the Academy."

Major Monogram fell quiet. He stared into space, remembering something from his past. Agent P dusted the cobwebs off his hat and then looked back up at the silent commander.

Major Monogram snapped back to reality.

He turned his attention to Agent P. "Anyway," he said, "Doofenshmirtz seems to be up to something. He's holed up at his evil woodland retreat. Your mission is to find out what he's up to."

Agent P didn't need to hear another word. With a spin of the captain's chair, he zoomed out of the briefing room. Major Monogram's face grew serious as he watched the platypus leave.

"Please, Agent P, be careful," he said in a

soft voice. He stared into space again. Tears welled in his eyes as a memory flooded back to him.

*"But I don't want to go to the Academy, Daddy,"* he had pleaded as a young boy.

*"I'm not your father, and it's been decided!"* a stern voice had replied.

*"I love you, Daddy,"* the young major had said.

Back in the present, Major Monogram wiped his eyes. This was no time for sentimental flashbacks, not when evil could be lurking around any corner. It was his job to keep the Tri-State Area safe, no matter what!

Back at Grandma and Grandpa's cabin, Phineas and Ferb's friends were all happily flying kites, playing ball, and running through the tall grass.

One of the visitors, however, was not a happy camper. At the edge of the clearing,

Candace lay with her head resting on a log. Flies buzzed annoyingly around her.

"You pesky bugs!" she snapped, swatting them away. "I'm trying to tan here!"

"Hey, Candace!" Phineas called, walking up to her. He was carrying a glass of green liquid. "I thought I'd bring my favorite camp counselor a 'Phineas Special.'"

"That is just a glass of limeade—and I am not a camp counselor!" Candace scoffed.

Before Phineas could reply, Isabella walked up to them. She was holding her trusty Fireside Girls clipboard. "Hey, Phineas," she said, "the girls have finished pitching the tents."

Isabella pointed behind her, where six Fireside Girls saluted proudly in front of their perfectly constructed tents.

"Can you sign here for our Tent Pitching patches, please?" Isabella asked.

"Sure thing!" Phineas replied. He signed the form on the clipboard.

"What are you doing?" Candace asked.

"Well, as camp director, I'd say I'm doing my job," Phineas replied with a satisfied smile.

"Gather 'round, kids!" Grandpa Clyde suddenly called from the other side of the glen. All the kids stopped their activities and ran to where he was. Grandpa Clyde had an excited gleam in his eye. "There's an old legend," he began, "about the 'Sasquatch.' A race of giant, hairy creatures living up here in these very woods!"

"Oooh!" the kids gasped.

"If my memory serves," Grandpa Clyde said, rubbing his chin thoughtfully, "I think there was a song written about it."

"Really?" Isabella asked eagerly. "Do you remember any of it?"

Grandpa Clyde whipped out a banjo and sang to the kids all about the legend of Bigfoot. He told them about the monster's long claws

and sharp teeth, and about how it would roam the woods at night looking for tasty children to eat. Grandpa Clyde finished his tale by warning the kids that Bigfoot could be watching them—at that very moment.

"Boo!" Grandpa Clyde cried.

"Aaaahh!" all the campers screamed in delight.

Phineas and Ferb laughed along with their friends. Suddenly, Phineas turned to Ferb and gave his brother a knowing look. Grandpa's story had given Phineas an idea. And if it worked out the way Phineas hoped, by the end of the night his friends would remember this trip as one of the most legendary summer campouts ever!

# Chapter THREE

ater that night, as the full moon rose over the mountains, Agent P sped through the sky on his high-tech hang glider. He stealthily landed on the roof of Dr. Doofenshmirtz's woodland hideout and crept across to the open skylight. Peering over the edge, Agent P could see the evil scientist typing furiously on his computer.

The platypus carefully lowered himself

through the skylight on a rope, just in time to hear Dr. Doofenshmirtz cackle, "Tonight! It all happens tonight!"

Agent P whipped out his binoculars to get a better look at the computer monitor. But he accidentally dropped them! Startled by the sound, Dr. Doofenshmirtz spun around.

"Perry the Platypus!" he said with a devious smile. "How unexpected. And by 'unexpected,' I mean . . ." The doctor frowned.

"Uh . . . unexpected. What are you doing here? This is my week off."

Agent P glanced at the center of the room. There was a table set with fine china and three gleaming candles. Two chairs sat on either side, which was strange, since

Dr. Doofenshmirtz usually dined alone.

"Oh, that?" Dr. Doofenshmirtz laughed nervously. "Well, uh, I suppose you should know. I started dating again. I met someone online. I know what you're thinking, but we're meeting tonight for the first time, and I—"

Agent P didn't need, or want, to hear another word. He lowered himself to the floor and quickly headed toward the door.

"Oh, you gotta go?" Dr. Doofenshmirtz

asked. He was unable to keep the relief out of his voice.

Suddenly, the doorbell rang!

"Oh, no, Perry the Platypus!" the evil doctor gasped. "She can't see you! She doesn't know I have a nemesis." He glanced at his watch. "Oh, and I don't think I have time to destroy you." He looked around the room desperately. "Ah! You can be my pet!" he said to Agent P. "Do you think you could act like a mindless animal?"

Agent P narrowed his eyes. But it was too late to come up with an alternate plan. The front door was already opening. A woman with short brown hair and thick glasses walked in.

"Oh, uh, hello?" she said, sounding unsure. "I'm looking for 'Strudelcutie 4427'?"

She glanced up from the paper in her hand and saw Agent P—now disguised as Perry the Platypus—on the floor.

"Well, aren't you the cutest little thing!" she

cooed, leaning down to pick him up. "Are you my date for this evening?"

"No!" exclaimed Dr. Doofenshmirtz. Then he tried to laugh. "No, no. That would be me. I'm 'Strudelcutie 4427.' Nice to meet you. Uh, this is my pet platypus. He was just going outside for a nightly walk."

"Oh, could I hold him a little longer?" the woman asked, giving Agent P a cuddle. "He's so sweet. Oh, yes! Yes, you are!"

"Well, I guess he can stay a little bit." Dr. Doofenshmirtz tapped his fingers together nervously. "But you know what they say . . . three's a crowd and whatnot." The doctor tried to laugh it off, but he had a bad feeling about this. His date had already wandered off, cradling Agent P in her arms like he was a little baby!

Things were not going as he had planned.

## Chapter FOUR

**B**ack in the woods, all the kids, along with Grandpa Clyde and Grandma Betty Joe, sat in a circle around a roaring campfire.

"So, Grandpa," Phineas asked, "what should we do? Tell scary stories? I've got one!"

"Oh, Phineas, you always start," Grandpa Clyde said. "Why not give another kid a chance?"

"Yes!" agreed Grandma Betty Joe. "How about you, Candace?"

"No," Candace said flatly.

"Okay . . ." Grandpa Clyde said. "Anyone else? Baljeet?"

"W-what?" Baljeet stammered anxiously, his eyes wide. "Uh, uh . . . oh . . . thank you." Someone handed him a flashlight. Baljeet held it under his chin so that it cast a spooky shadow across his face. "Well, this is a story about a kid who comes to this country and goes to camp."

Buford, sitting right next to Baljeet, glared at the boy. It made Baljeet even more nervous!

"He, like, has to share a tent with the bully," Baljeet continued. "It's really quite terrifying, actually. Quite terrifying."

Everyone waited for Baljeet to continue his story. But after a moment, they realized that he was finished. There was an awkward pause, filled by the sound of chirping crickets.

"Take it away, Phineas!" Grandpa Clyde finally said.

Phineas leaped into action. This was the moment he'd been waiting for.

"All right, Grandpa. I've got a good one!" Phineas announced. "It's about Bigfoot!"

"Bigfoot?" echoed the Fireside Girls.

"Bigfoot?" cried Buford.

"Bigfoot!" Grandma Betty Joe exclaimed in Candace's ear.

"Grandma!" shouted Candace.

"Sorry, dear," Grandma Betty Joe replied.

Phineas couldn't wait. He jumped right into the creepiest, most nail-biting tale of Bigfoot that his friends had ever heard. He told them about the last time the creature had been seen and about the hikers who were unfortunate enough to cross the monster's path. Despite the light from the flickering campfire, the darkness around the kids seemed to grow deeper as Phineas continued his tale. Somewhere in the distance a lone wolf howled.

"And they say that when the moon is full,

like it is tonight . . ." Phineas dropped his voice to a hush, "Bigfoot will return and exact his revenge."

Just then, there was a rustle in the woods.

"What was that noise?" Phineas gasped.

At that moment, four huge, hairy beasts sprang out of the bushes! Their long arms waved in the air. Their sharp claws glinted in the moonlight, and their eyes glowed red.

"Aaaahhhh!" screamed all of the campers. Buford even jumped right into Baljeet's arms!

As his friends ran around in a panic, Phineas doubled over with laughter. "You guys crack me up!" he cried, slapping his knee.

"Phineas, what are you talking about?" Isabella asked from her hiding place behind a log. Ferb was sitting on the same log, but he was strangely motionless.

"There's no Bigfoot!" Phineas exclaimed, still laughing. He turned on his flashlight and aimed it at the shadowy forest. "It's just Ferb in the tree. Look!"

Everyone turned to where he was pointing. Sure enough, Ferb was perched high in the tree, working a complicated set of levers and pulleys attached to fake monsters.

"See?" Phineas said. "They're just dummies! Nice rope skills, my friend!"

In the flashlight's glow, everyone could see that the horrible beasts were nothing more than potato sacks clumsily stitched together to look like monsters. A series of strings

connected them to the puppet controls that Ferb was working from the tree.

"Then who is this?" Isabella asked nervously, looking at the identical Ferb sitting next to her on the log.

"Ah, it's an inflatable Ferb," Phineas explained as he walked over. He popped open a valve on the dummy's nose. There was a long *hisssss* of escaping air, and the fake Ferb deflated.

"That was awesome!" Buford said from Baljeet's arms.

Phineas and Ferb exchanged a grin. If even Buford was scared, then their spooky prank had been more successful than they had dared to dream!

**B**ack at Dr. Doofenshmirtz's evil mountain retreat, his date had gone from bad to worse. His lady friend was now completely ignoring him, focusing all of her attention on Agent P.

"You are the cutest thing I have ever seen!" she cooed, gently petting Agent P. "Yes, you are. Yes, you are."

"You know, some people say we look alike," Dr. Doofenshmirtz chimed in, hoping to get the evening back on track.

His date cast a sideways glance at him. "Yeah, I don't think so," she replied, shaking her head vigorously. "Not at all. No, not at all." She held Agent P close to her face and gave him an extra nuzzle.

"Uh, darling, you haven't even touched your cucumber water," Dr. Doofenshmirtz tried again. "I made it especially for you."

But his date just kept petting Agent P. "You know, 'Strudelcutie 4427' was a lot less needy online . . ." she said to the platypus as she rubbed him against her cheek. "Oh, yes. Yes, he was."

Dr. Doofenshmirtz sighed in frustration. "I'm going to get some air," he said, disappointed.

"A lot less needy online!" his date repeated to Agent P as Dr. Doofenshmirtz walked away.

Out on the balcony, the evil doctor took a big gulp of cucumber water. He gagged and spit it out over the wall. "Oh, I don't even like cucumbers!" he groaned. "Why do I always get the crazies?"

Suddenly, Dr. Doofenshmirtz heard screams echoing from deep in the forest. His face brightened.

"That sounded like screaming children!" he said excitedly. He hopped onto the balcony wall so that he could hear better. He had no way of knowing that the cries were coming from Phineas and Ferb's friends, right after the boys had played their Bigfoot prank.

"But today's not my birthday . . ." Dr. Doofenshmirtz said thoughtfully. He leaned

as far over as he could to try and figure out where the noise was coming from.

Suddenly, he lost his balance! "Whoa—whoa!" Dr. Doofenshmirtz wobbled on the ledge. Then he plunged over the side!

"Aaaahhhh!" he cried as he fell far down the mountain. He crashed through leaves and branches all the way to the bottom before finally landing with a loud *thump*.

But his date was too preoccupied to notice.

She was still inside, squeezing the helpless Agent P.

It took Dr. Doofenshmirtz a long while to untangle himself from the prickly overgrowth. In the end, he couldn't free himself from all the thorns and weeds. So he climbed back up the wall wearing a head-to-toe suit of stringy vines and branches.

Dr. Doofenshmirtz grunted and groaned as he climbed back up the steep wall.

"What was that?" his date asked in alarm. She looked down at the cuddly platypus. "You'd better stay here while I investigate."

She gently placed Agent P on the couch and walked over to the balcony. What she saw made her eyes grow wide in fear. A terrible, leaf-covered creature was climbing over the balcony wall!

"Bigfoot?" Dr. Doofenshmirtz's date gasped.

"Huh? What?" the doctor spluttered through the weeds covering his mouth.

His date's eyes grew angry. "BIGFOOT!" She ran to grab her oversized purse and rushed back onto the balcony.

"No, no, no! Wait! It's me, St—" Dr. Doofenshmirtz tried to say, holding up his hands.

But his date was the kind of person who acted first and asked questions later. She swung her heavy bag at him.

*Wham!*

"Ooof—whoa—whah—ahh—ugh!" Dr. Doofenshmirtz howled as he bounced back down the mountainside and into the trees below.

His date raised her eyebrows. Something about the creature's voice sounded familiar. She walked to the edge and peered over the side. "Strudelcutie 4427?" she asked. "Oops."

Meanwhile, Agent P took full advantage of the distraction to make his escape. He strapped on his parachute and took a running leap off the roof, gliding away to safety.

The platypus gave a huge sigh of relief. Being smothered by Dr. Doofenshmirtz's date was almost worse than being caught in one of the evil scientist's traps. He was lucky to have made it out in one piece.

Still, there was the satisfaction of knowing that Dr. Doofenshmirtz hadn't been planning a diabolical plot after all. But that didn't mean Agent P could take it easy. In fact, he had a feeling that Dr. Doofenshmirtz was going to be in such a bad mood from his dating debacle that his next plan could be one of his worst ever.

And when that happened . . . Agent P would be ready!

## Chapter SIX

**B**ack at the campsite, Phineas and Ferb's friends were still laughing from the brothers' scary practical joke.

"Whoo-hoo!" Grandpa Clyde chuckled. "That was a good one, boys. You sure got us!"

Candace, however, was very angry. She threw up her arms in frustration. "I can't take it anymore!" she yelled.

"It was just a joke, Candace," Phineas said.

"You're a joke, Phineas!" Candace shot back.

"Candace, honey, calm down," Grandpa Clyde said right away.

"Calm down?" Candace repeated, shouting at the top of her lungs. "I don't want to calm down!"

"But your screaming might attract a real bigfoot," Phineas pointed out.

"A real bigfoot?" she mocked him. "Oh, give it a rest, Phineas! Everyone knows there's no such thing as a real—"

Suddenly, Candace had a creepy feeling that something was standing right behind her. She slowly turned around . . . and came face-to-face with an enormous beast! It had massive muscles and tangled brown fur. Razor-sharp claws curved from the tips of its fingers. Its evil red eyes glinted in the moonlight, and its mouth opened wide to reveal gigantic, pointy fangs!

But Candace just rolled her eyes. "Oh, fine!"

she said. "What's this one made of? Popsicle sticks and glitter?"

"Uh . . . no . . ." Phineas stammered. All the kids around the campfire backed away slowly.

Everyone except Candace. She looked the bigfoot up and down as it roared. "Huh," she said.

Then, the horrifying creature grabbed Candace and popped her into its mouth!

"Aaaaaaahhhhh!" she screamed as it started to chomp on her. Everyone cried out in terror as they caught a glimpse of Candace's

arm—then her leg—then her head inside the monster's mouth!

All the campers fled, hiding in the woods

as best they could. Only Grandma Betty Joe and Grandpa Clyde remained in the clearing, clinging to each other.

Slowly, the bigfoot approached them. Then, Grandpa Clyde snickered. "Looks like we fooled 'em, Ma!" he said.

*Zip!* A hidden zipper running down the bigfoot's belly opened, and Grandma Betty Joe

poked her head out. "Did you see the look on their faces?" She laughed.

Candace peeked out, too. "That was so cool!" she said as she crawled out of the enormous costume.

"Good one!" agreed Grandma Betty Joe.

"And you got an inflatable grandma, too," Candace said as she walked over to the log where Grandpa Clyde was sitting. Next to him was Grandma Betty Joe's double.

"Oh, I'm not inflatable," the double said.

"I'm your grandma's identical twin. I only come out once a year when these two want to prank someone. Well, back to my closet!"

"See ya next year, Lorraine!" Grandma Betty Joe said as she waved to her sister. She started laughing again. "Come on, let's round up those scared kids and have some hot cocoa."

As Candace, Grandma, and Grandpa headed into the woods to track down all the scattered, screaming campers, there was one cry that didn't belong to a child. It came from Dr. Doofenshmirtz. His second tumble off the balcony was far worse than the first. Instead of landing in the patch of brambles, he continued to roll head over heels down the rocky mountainside. Finally, he fell facedown in the mud.

He groaned heavily as he got up and started to brush himself off. "It's not the worst date I've ever had," he said, trying to look on the bright side. "There was that one that kept stabbing me with a fork. . . ."

Dr. Doofenshmirtz frowned as he stood up. He seemed to be tangled in some sort of string. The doctor shook his arms, muttering. "Get this off of—" he started to say.

As Dr. Doofenshmirtz struggled, four enormous bigfoot puppets rose from the bushes. He had no way of knowing that he had fallen right through Ferb's complicated contraption, and was now controlling the bigfoot dummies with his every move! He ran for his life, dragging

the bigfoots along behind him. As he fled into the night, he realized that this was, in fact, the very worst date he'd ever had.

**A** little while later, all the campers were gathered on the porch of Grandma and Grandpa's cabin, sipping hot cocoa. Candace stood in front of the other kids. She couldn't stop laughing.

"I sure got you guys!" she gloated. She put her hands on her hips. "You should've seen your faces! Only unsophisticated brains would believe in monsters. Yes, it takes a mature adult, such as myself, to know that there's no such thing as . . . "

Just then, Candace's voice trailed off as she spotted something terrible running behind the other kids. It was the leaf-covered Dr. Doofenshmirtz racing past, followed by four huge monsters!

"BIGFOOT!" Candace screamed. She dashed into the cabin, slamming the door behind her.

The other campers turned. By that point, Dr. Doofenshmirtz had passed the clearing. All the friends saw was the full moon gleaming down on the forest.

"Oh, I do not believe her one bit," Baljeet said, shaking his head.

All the kids echoed their agreement. Ferb slurped his hot chocolate as Perry climbed onto Phineas's lap. "Hey, Perry," Phineas

said. Then he gave the platypus a closer look. "Why are you all covered in lipstick?"

Perry just made his funny chittering noise. He could never tell Phineas the real reason he was covered in kiss marks. It would completely blow his cover as a secret agent.

Plus, he'd rather die of embarrassment than admit to an evening of cuddles with Dr. Doofenshmirtz's date! The platypus sighed. After tonight's adventure, he decided that there were far worse things to be afraid of than a bigfoot in the woods.

# Part TWO

The golden sun was just peeking over the mountains at Camp Phineas and Ferb. All the kids were still fast asleep in their tents. Suddenly, a bugle blasted out a wake-up call. Phineas bolted upright in his sleeping bag.

"It sounds like somebody's strangling a cat!" he gasped. He then smiled broadly at his brother, Ferb. "It must be Grandpa!"

Ferb stretched and yawned. Even their pet platypus, Perry, couldn't sleep another wink with that dreadful racket. Phineas charged outside, ready for another awesome summer day in the great outdoors.

"Wakey-wakey, eggs and bakey!" Phineas called as he slapped on a green camping hat.

Baljeet stumbled out of the tent next door, coughing uncontrollably. "I cannot believe we eat the same food!" Baljeet complained to Buford, who also came out from the tent.

In response, Buford burped. The smell was gross! "Believe it," Buford grunted as he walked away.

Nearby, Candace emerged from her tent, wearing a purple bathrobe and fuzzy slippers. Her arms were full of fluffy towels, fancy shampoo, and a special scrubbing brush.

"Grandma, would you show me where the shower is?" she asked.

"Shower? Why, sure, honey," Grandma Betty Joe replied. "Would you like a massage and a fruity drink, too? How about a manicure and a mud facial while you lay by the pool

eating crab cakes?" Her grandma chuckled and walked away.

"I can do without the sarcasm!" Candace called after her, waving the bath brush in the air.

All the campers gathered around the campfire for breakfast. Grandpa Clyde piled steaming eggs and crispy bacon onto the hungry kids' plates.

As the kids ate, Grandpa Clyde announced their day's activity. "Time for our nature walk to Badbeard Lake," he said.

"Why do they call it Badbeard Lake?" Phineas asked curiously.

"Well, it's a body of freshwater surrounded by land—" Grandpa Clyde began.

"No, the 'Badbeard' part," Phineas said.

"Oh, right," Grandpa Clyde replied. "It was named after Badbeard, the most ruthless freshwater pirate ever to plunder a lakeside community."

"Cool!" all the campers echoed together.

"And in the middle of Badbeard Lake lies Spleen Island," Grandpa Clyde continued, "where legend has it, Badbeard buried his bountiful booty!"

"Treasure?" gasped the kids.

"Aye, mateys," Grandpa Clyde said in his best pirate accent. He whipped a black marker out of his pocket and colored in one lens of his eyeglasses so it looked like he was wearing an eye patch. "Arrr!" he growled.

Phineas raised his eyebrows. "Why are you

talking like a pirate, Grandpa?" he asked.

"Argh! I'm trying to tell the story of Badbeard the Pirate," Grandpa replied. "Meet me at the trailhead in five minutes."

"Aye, aye, Captain Grandpa!" the campers said, saluting.

"That's the spirit!" Grandpa Clyde cried. He turned and headed down to the trail.

Just then, Baljeet pulled his overalls out and peeked inside. "Oh, dear," he sighed. "I seem to be missing my underpants."

"Heh-heh-heh-heh-heh!" Buford chuckled, pointing at the top of a nearby flagpole. Earlier that morning, he had scoured the entire campgrounds and found the one and only flagpole in the area. Now, a pair of pale yellow boxer shorts with orange polka dots swayed gently in the breeze. Baljeet sighed. He would have to go back to the tent for fresh underpants. Again.

After breakfast, all the campers gathered their things and walked through the woods to meet Grandpa Clyde.

"So you see, kids?" Grandpa explained as he led them on their early-morning nature walk. "Wherever you go, the forest is teeming with life for us to step on. Remember, always stick to the trails so you won't get lost. And whatever you do, never touch the orange moss that grows on the right side of the Joom-Joom tree."

"Boring," Candace said from the back of the group. She pulled out her pink cell phone. "I'm calling Stacy."

As Grandpa Clyde continued speaking, Candace put her hand on a nearby tree trunk. She didn't notice the strange orange moss covering it.

"I can't get any reception up here!" she complained, flipping her phone shut.

"So steer clear of the moss," Grandpa Clyde repeated to the campers. "The slightest touch, and it will absorb through the skin, causing wild hallucinations!"

Candace rolled her eyes and turned around.

Just then, she realized she was leaning up against a moss-covered tree. "Huh?" she cried, yanking her palm away. Her skin was covered in velvety orange moss.

"Oh, no!" Candace gasped. She panicked and shook her hand. "Was that the right side or the wrong side?"

Candace backed up as far as she could from the tree . . . only to bump into *another* tree that was also covered in the dangerous orange moss. It no longer mattered which side of the tree was right or wrong; she'd touched both!

Candace screamed and ran away. Meanwhile, the rest of the campers had reached the steps leading to a large lake. It was crystal blue and had a big island in the center.

"There she blows, mateys—Badbeard Lake," Grandpa Clyde announced, pointing with his walking stick.

"Ooh," echoed the campers.

"And there be Spleen Island," Grandpa Clyde continued in his pirate accent. "The bones of them that hunted the treasure all be lying below in Davy Jones's locker."

"Cool!" exclaimed Phineas.

"Let's go!" Grandpa Clyde led the excited kids down the rickety stairway to the lake. Just then, Grandma Betty Joe realized one of the campers was missing. "Candace?" she called, looking around. "Where's Candace?"

But there was no response. Candace was long gone.

**M**eanwhile, back at the campsite, Perry the Platypus had slapped on his fedora and transformed into Agent P. He whipped out a remote control and pressed the red button on top. Major Monogram had given him this top secret device so that he would be able to access his hidden lair from anywhere in the Tri-State Area.

What Agent P wasn't sure of was the mode

of transportation the remote would provide. Without warning, a fierce eagle swooped down from the sky and snatched Agent P in its talons!

The startled platypus struggled to get away. But it was no use. The enormous bird carried Agent P straight to its nest and dropped him down in the center. Agent P was just about to try to escape when, unexpectedly, the eagle donned a fedora of his own. The bird was actually Agent E. Agent P sighed in relief. He knew that O.W.C.A.'s methods of transportation required secrecy. But he never expected to travel by talon!

One of the eggs in the center of the nest cracked open. Inside it, a small monitor broadcast an image of Major Monogram. "Good morning, Agent P," the commander began. "And thank you for your help, Agent E. Sorry if we alarmed you, Agent P. We're remodeling our regular base here. Actually, my wife's doing it Mexican-country style. Heh, distressed wood and wrought iron. Should all be very . . . "

Agents P and E exchanged a glance. When Major Monogram started talking about decor, it was hard to get him back on track. But Agent E had an idea. He bent toward the monitor with a beak full of wiggly worms!

"Whoa! Hey, Agent E, back off!" Major Monogram exclaimed. The worms had startled him. But at least he was focused on the mission again. "Uh, anyway," he said to

Agent P, "Dr. Doofenshmirtz has been spotted on Spleen Island. He's moving boxes and equipment into what's known as the Haunted Cave of the Old Sea Hag. Honestly, I'm not making this stuff up. Anyway, we believe he's creating a new hideout there. We want you to foil his plans. Good luck, Agent P."

The platypus saluted. He knew it was his mission to stop the evil Dr. Doofenshmirtz at all costs.

But little did the platypus know that a short distance away, Candace was watching him!

"No way. This is so weird!" Candace chuckled. She was perched in a tall tree across from the nest where Agent P was being briefed. Because she had touched the orange moss, Candace thought she was hallucinating!

"I see Perry with an eagle and they're both dressed like secret agents and they're talking to a man inside an egg. That is so messed up." Candace giggled.

Then she gasped. "Hey, wait a minute. How did I get way up here?" She looked down and realized, for the first time, just how high up in the tree she was. She cried out and flailed her arms like wings before tumbling out of the tree, hitting every branch on her way down to the ground. Luckily, there was a thick pile of soft green leaves at the bottom to help break her fall. Candace sat up, her hair tangled and her clothes covered in mud.

But none of that really bothered her. Thanks

to the orange moss she was in a very silly mood. She knew that everything she was seeing must be a hallucination. Just then, Agent E swooped overhead, carrying Agent P in his talons. Candace watched as he dropped the secret-agent platypus onto a pier at the edge of Badbeard Lake. The agents saluted each other. Then the eagle soared away. Quickly, Agent P jumped onto a Wet Ski.

"Now Perry has a Wet Ski?" Candace asked in amazement. "How strange can this get?"

Around her, the sky suddenly went swirly. A zebra in a rocking chair appeared next to her.

"Oh, it gets much stranger, Kevin," the zebra said to Candace.

Candace was about to reply when a rope from Agent P's Wet Ski accidentally coiled around her ankle. It dragged her into the choppy waters of Badbeard Lake.

And as Agent P zoomed across the waves, Candace found herself going along for the ride!

## Chapter THREE

On the sandy shores of Badbeard Lake, Phineas and his friends checked out Grandpa's old rowboat. "Hey, I know what we should do today," Phineas exclaimed. "Let's be real pirates and go find Badbeard's treasure!"

"Sure, knock yourselves out," Grandpa Clyde said, laughing. "I was just about your age when I first heard about Badbeard's treasure. I'd come up here every summer and

search for it. I felt drawn by the excitement and adventure. Of course, then I discovered girls and the rest is a blur. I never found the treasure, but I did find a treasure map."

Grandpa Clyde took off his ranger hat and pulled out a tattered roll of parchment that was hidden inside.

"Treasure map?" Buford asked.

"But be warned, mateys," Grandpa continued, speaking in his bad pirate accent again. "They say Badbeard's treasure comes with a curse."

"A curse?" the campers echoed, their eyes wide.

"Aye! Them who disturb the treasure of Badbeard shall be cursed with bad beards for the rest of their days," Grandpa Clyde cautioned.

"You mean, we'll be stuck with big, ugly beards on our faces for the rest of our lives?" Phineas asked.

"That's gnarly!" Buford piped up.

"Well, while you kids search for treasure, I'd better go search for Grandma," Grandpa Clyde said in his normal voice. "I wish there was a map for that. . . ."

As Grandpa Clyde wandered off, the kids crowded around Phineas. He carefully unrolled the parchment and hung it up so everyone could see.

The map was yellowed with age and had

small tears along its edges, but the drawings were still sharp. At the top was a picture of Badbeard himself, alongside an image of a locked treasure chest and a pirate ship with billowing sails. In the lower left corner, there was a compass to indicate directions. And in the center, there was a giant, detailed diagram of Badbeard Lake and Spleen Island.

Phineas pointed to a dotted line that showed how to find the treasure. "Okay, troops," he said. "We set sail from Point Plots, head through the Stones of Gall and into the Cove of Incontinence. And then we continue on foot into the dark Tunnel of Doom!" He paused for effect. "Well, that sounds delightful. And X marks the spot. First thing we've got to do is remake Grandpa's secondhand dinghy into a first-rate pirate ship. Ferb, any ideas?" Phineas asked.

Ferb hopped off the log he was sitting on and held up a tiny piece of paper. He then unfolded it again and again until he had a diagram that was almost the size of a house!

"Whoa," Phineas said. "Impressive."

The diagram showed how to build a massive boat Ferb had designed himself. With these plans, the kids were guaranteed to create the greatest pirate ship ever to sail Badbeard Lake.

Quickly, the campers got to work. They were all determined to find Badbeard's treasure—even if it meant being cursed with bad beards for the rest of their lives!

**A**ll morning the kids sawed, nailed, and banged away until their pirate ship was ready. Afterward, Phineas donned a pirate hat and a dashing royal-blue naval coat. Ferb tied a spotted green kerchief around his head, while Buford whittled a fake wooden leg for himself. Isabella put on a fitted jacket and an oversize captain's hat with a feather in one side. As the friends set sail onto the lake, they all

looked like they could have been members of Badbeard's original pirate crew.

Soon, they neared the shore of Spleen Island. Phineas, Ferb, Isabella, Baljeet, and Buford climbed aboard a rowboat. Together they paddled over to the shore and hiked up a rocky trail.

Finally, the friends reached the entrance to a large cave. "This is it: the Tunnel of Doom!" Phineas said excitedly. "Just like on the map."

He led them into the cave and through its winding passages.

"Are you sure we're going the right way?" Isabella asked worriedly

"Sure, I'm sure," Phineas told her. "We just follow Ferb. He's got the map!"

Suddenly, a gust of wind blew through the cave. It ripped the map from Ferb's hands.

"Uh-oh . . ." Phineas said. The map fluttered down a chasm so deep they couldn't even see the bottom.

"Oh, well." Phineas shrugged. "I'm sure it's pretty straightforward from here." The

kids looked out over the gorge. A rickety rope bridge was the only way across.

"It doesn't look very safe," Isabella said.

"I think you'd better test it," added Buford.

Phineas was happy to do so. He gingerly walked out to the middle of the bridge. "No problem!" he said cheerfully. "It'll hold us."

Convinced that the bridge was safe, his friends crowded onto it. A look of panic crossed Phineas's face. "No, wait! Not all at once!" he cried.

But it was too late. The ropes at one end of the bridge snapped, and the kids somersaulted through the air. They plunged into a pool of water deep inside the cave, and landed on something slimy and green.

It was a sea monster!

"Run for it!" Phineas shouted as the sea monster lifted its head and opened its jaws. Its mouth was full of sharp, scary-looking teeth!

The campers ran as fast as they could over precarious rock ledges and narrow stone

bridges. As soon as they felt they were safe from the sea monster, they slowed down a little. They found themselves in the innermost tunnels of Spleen Island. The passages were dark and spooky, with flickering shadows and unearthly noises.

"This place is creeping me out," Baljeet said in a quavering voice.

"Phineas, we're not getting lost, are we?" Isabella asked nervously.

"Yeah," snapped Buford. "What if there is no treasure?"

"Perhaps the real treasure is true friend-ship and the spirit of adventure," Baljeet suggested.

No one said anything for a moment.

"Nah," Phineas finally replied. He pointed to a stone archway that was crowned with a skull and crossbones. An enormous red X was painted on a pair of wooden doors. "There it is, over there. X marks the spot!"

Together, the campers pushed open the heavy doors. Inside, they saw a treasure chest sitting on top of a pile of bones.

"Look, there's the chest," Isabella exclaimed.

"But who will dare open it?" asked Baljeet.

"I'll open it," Phineas volunteered eagerly.

"But Phineas, what about the curse?" Isabella said, worried.

"Bad beards forever, dude," Buford reminded him.

"And you don't even have a chin!" Baljeet
added.

"That's a chance I'll have to take," Phineas
said as he and Ferb approached the chest.
Carefully, Phineas creaked open the lid and
peered inside.

"Shiver me timbers," Phineas gasped. All
his friends held their breath as their fearless
leader looked deep into the chest.

"The curse is true," Phineas said. "We will
have bad beards forever!"

When he turned around, half of Phineas's

face was covered by an unruly black beard that spilled down his chest.

"Oh, no!" shouted the other campers.

Phineas laughed. "But it's full of bad *fake* beards!" he said, lifting out two handfuls from the trunk. There were brown beards and blond beards, red beards and gray beards. There was even a checkered beard.

With a loud cheer, the other kids rushed toward the chest. This was the gnarliest pirate booty they could have hoped for!

**U**naware of her brothers' adventure on Spleen Island, Candace bounced across the choppy waves of Badbeard Lake. But she wasn't traveling by boat. Her foot was still tangled in the rope of Agent P's Wet Ski.

Under normal circumstances, Candace would have been terrified. But the orange moss had made her so loopy that she wasn't afraid at all. A happy grin was plastered across her face as she sped through the water, algae and weeds clinging to her hair.

Meanwhile, Agent P didn't realize that he had a stowaway attached to the Wet Ski. He expertly piloted the vehicle into the Haunted Cave of the Old Sea Hag in the heart of Spleen Island. When Agent P stopped, Candace untangled herself from the rope and climbed onto a rock. She watched curiously as Agent P headed for a large steel door. Then she giggled. This was the wackiest thing she had ever seen!

Agent P flung the heavy door open and raced through, prepared to find out once and for all what the diabolical Dr. Doofenshmirtz was up to. But before he could defend himself, a giant metallic claw descended from the roof of the cave and grabbed him!

"Is that the cable guy?" Dr. Doofenshmirtz called out from the other room. He strode in, his nose buried in a television guide. "So, Mr. Cable Man, you don't carry the Evil Science channel? What's up with—" Dr. Doofenshmirtz stopped abruptly when he saw Agent P dangling from the ceiling.

"Perry the Platypus! Oh, give me a break. I'm moving . . . legally! I bought this place."

Dr. Doofenshmirtz gestured at the grand cave around them. It was filled with electronic gadgets and evil-looking contraptions. "And cheap, too," the doctor added proudly. "It's supposed to be haunted by a terrifying old sea hag." He chuckled. "Look, Perry the Platypus, just because *I'm* evil doesn't mean everything I *do* is evil."

Agent P crossed his arms and narrowed his eyes at Dr. Doofenshmirtz. It was clear that he didn't believe a word the devious doctor had said.

"Fine! You want evil, Perry the Platypus?" the doctor demanded. "I'll give you evil!"

A malicious gleam came to the doctor's eyes as the metallic claw whisked Agent P over to an ominous-looking trapdoor. Then Dr. Doofenshmirtz picked up a remote control. "Now, Perry the Platypus, why don't you say hello to my new pet crocodiles?" He pressed the red button on the remote and laughed as

a trapdoor beneath Agent P slid open. Two fierce crocodiles leaped out of the water, snapping at Agent P's feet!

"Meet Susan and Susan," Dr. Doofenshmirtz exclaimed. "I named them after each other. Now, prepare to be delicious!"

Just then, Candace—still covered in algae and suffering from the effects of the orange moss—wandered over. She cackled in a shrill voice. She was so out of it that she thought this was all a wild hallucination.

"The sea hag!" Dr. Doofenshmirtz gasped, pointing at Candace.

"A pharmacist!" Candace cried, looking back at him.

Dr. Doofenshmirtz stumbled backward. But he accidentally fell right into the crocodile pit! The remote control flew out of his hand. One of the buttons hit the stone floor, freeing Agent P from the metal claw.

Agent P was just about to escape when

Candace suddenly called, "Hey, Perry!" She was standing next to the giant self-destruct mechanism Dr. Doofenshmirtz had installed in the wall. "I'm going to get a snack from the vending machine," she said. "You want something?"

In her orange-moss daze, Candace thought the self-destruct box was a food dispenser!

Agent P waved his hands frantically, but Candace didn't get it. "Suit yourself," she said with a shrug. She punched the large red button. "I'm having some beef jerky."

An alarm immediately rang out and a robotic voice announced, "Island self-destruct sequence activated."

Agent P leaped into action. He scrambled across the cave and grabbed Candace, dragging her to safety just as massive boulders started to fall.

"Wait, my beef jerky!" Candace cried.

Meanwhile, Dr. Doofenshmirtz was still struggling to get free from the crocodile pit.

"Ach!" he cried. "Someone always finds my self-destruct button. Oh, curse you, Perry the Platypus, blah, blah, blah." In truth, Dr. Doofenshmirtz's heart wasn't really in it this time. He had bigger things to worry about. Like making sure he wasn't Susan and Susan's lunch!

# Chapter SIX

**O**ver on the other side of the island, Phineas, Ferb, and their friends were having a blast trying on all the fake beards.

"These are the best bad beards ever!" Phineas exclaimed.

Suddenly, the ground started to shake, and rocks fell around the kids. They didn't know it, but the self-destruct sequence Candace had activated was causing the whole island to sink.

99

"Quick, grab as many beards as you can carry and let's get out of here!" Phineas cried.

With their arms full of pirate booty, the campers raced through the cave, dodging boulders that plunged from the ceiling.

The sea monster at the entrance to the Tunnel of Doom was waiting for them with its mouth open wide. But the friends escaped through a different passageway. The monster charged after them and got stuck in a narrow tunnel. Once outside, the campers leaped into

their rowboat, and Phineas held his wooden sword high.

"Cast off," he ordered, just like a real captain. "Put your backs into it, mateys!" They bounced across the lake as fast as they could, heading toward their ship.

Back inside the cave, Agent P gripped Candace's hand as he dragged her through the winding tunnels. Together, they tumbled down a waterfall into the churning waves of Badbeard Lake.

"Wheee!" Candace cried happily, as if she

**101**

were zooming down a waterslide. Just before they hit the bottom, Agent E swooped down to rescue them both! He flew over Phineas and Ferb's pirate ship, dropping Candace and Agent P safely into the crow's nest before anyone noticed him.

From the deck of the pirate ship, everyone watched in amazement as Spleen Island sank into the lake.

"Oh, man," said Buford.

"Whoa," gasped Isabella.

None of the friends could believe it. They had made it out just in the nick of time.

After a moment, Phineas looked at Ferb. "Hey, by the way, where's Per—" he began.

But before he could finish his sentence, Agent P and Candace snuck down from the crow's nest and onto the deck. By the time Phineas turned around, Agent P had become Perry the Platypus once more.

"Oh, never mind," Phineas said.

"Hey, Perry, what happened to your cute little secret-agent hat?" Candace asked.

But Perry didn't answer. He just looked at her as though he were a normal pet platypus.

"Well, Ferb, me old matey, our first time out as pirates and we come home with a bounty of beards," Phineas said proudly as the pirate ship sailed back toward camp.

"And perhaps the greatest pirate story ever told," Ferb replied.

Later, when Grandpa Clyde heard the kids' tale of daring adventure, he had to agree. "Wow, that's the greatest pirate story ever told!" he exclaimed. The funny blue beard covering his face bounced up and down as he spoke. All of the campers grinned. They were each wearing their own special beard from the treasure chest.

Grandma Betty Joe, sporting a spiffy white beard, excused herself from the group to go check on Candace. She headed over to a tent where her granddaughter was snuggled up in a sleeping bag. "How are you feeling, honey?" she asked.

"Better. Thanks, Grandma," Candace replied with a smile from behind a shaggy brown beard. Even Perry the Platypus was wearing a short red beard!

"Can you believe I actually thought Perry was a secret agent?" Candace asked, shaking her head.

Perry made his chittering noise, grateful

that Candace thought everything she had seen was just a hallucination. If it hadn't been for the orange moss, his cover might really have been blown.

"Well, I learned my lesson," Candace continued. "Stay *away* from the orange moss."

"The orange moss?" Grandma Betty Joe asked, wrinkling her brow. "Is that what your grandpa said? Oh, he always gets that wrong. It's the blue moss you've got to watch out for."

"Wh-what?" Candace stammered. She sat up in her sleeping bag and put her hand on the ground for support.

"I guess it was all in your head." Grandma Betty Joe smiled. "You get some rest now, sweetie."

"The *blue* moss," Candace repeated. But how could that be? she wondered. If the orange moss didn't cause hallucinations, then did that mean . . . ?

Just then, she looked down at her hand and gasped. Blue moss was covering the ground right by her sleeping bag. And her hand was directly in it!

"What? Oh!" she cried.

But it was too late. Already the room around her was starting to spin.

"Love the beard, Kevin." The zebra had returned. He pointed a hoof in Candace's direction.

Candace closed her eyes and sighed. There

was nothing she could do but lie back and wait for the effects of the moss to wear off . . . again.

Outside, the other kids were laughing and pretending to have sword fights, all with their wonderfully bad beards in place. Phineas and Ferb were pretty pleased with how their pirate journey had turned out. They had built a mighty ship, tracked down a long-lost treasure, and escaped a sinking island, all in one day! If this was the sort of excitement that came from a simple morning nature walk, what amazing adventures awaited them tomorrow?

Only time would tell.

Don't miss the fun in the next
Phineas & Ferb book . . .

# The Sky's the Limit!

Adapted by Ellie O'Ryan
Based on the series created by Dan Povenmire & Jeff "Swampy" Marsh

It's a bird . . . it's a plane . . . it's Phineas
and Ferb in the biggest airplane in the world!
When the brothers decide to break the record
for the largest airplane ever built, their very
own jumbo jet leads to unexpected adventure
in the wild blue yonder. Then, Phineas
and Ferb invent an antigravity
machine, and Major
Monogram suspects
the boys are working
for Dr. Doofenshmirtz!